Disney

My First Stories

MOWGLI'S FIRST DANCE

pi kids ®

An imprint of Phoenix International Publications, Inc.

Chicago • London • New York • Hamburg • Mexico City • Sydney

Little Mowgli whistles a tune as he hurries along. There is someplace he needs to be.

Kaa hears Mowgli whistling. The snake slides up to him and says, "Scat-a-waddle-dee-do, I'll dance with you! We'll rattle and roll!"

"No, thanks," says Mowgli. "I've got to go!"

When Mowgli gets to the river,
Baloo bounces by and splashes him!
"You're in an awful hurry,
Little Britches," Baloo says.

"Hold on, Mowgli!" calls Baloo. "Scat-a-waddle-dee-do, I'll dance with you! We'll mambo!" "No, thanks," says Mowgli. "I've got to go!"

Suddenly, Mowgli hears a loud thump. Bagheera pounces off a rock and lands in front of him.

"Scat-a-waddle-dee-do, I'll dance with you!" calls the panther. "We'll do the stomp!"

"No, thanks," says Mowgli. "I've got to go!"

When Mowgli rushes by King Louie, the orangutan tries to stop him.

"Scat-a-waddle-dee-do,
I'll dance with you!" Louie shouts.
"We'll swing dance!"
    "No, thanks," says Mowgli.
"I've got to go!"

Mowgli is getting tired, but he keeps on going. Just then, Shere Khan jumps out of the grass to surprise him!

"Scat-a-waddle-dee-do, I'll dance with you!" growls Shere Khan. "We'll do the pounce!"

"No, thanks," says Mowgli. "I've got to go! I'm invited to a party!"

Mowgli sees his favorite spot in the distance.

"I'm almost there. I don't want to be late," he says as he starts to run.

When Mowgli arrives, his friends all welcome him! He looks at them and smiles.

"Scat-a-waddle-dee-do, now I'll dance with all of you!" shouts Mowgli.